MW01658246

CAUTION THIN ICE

Caution: Thin Ice

Poems by
Lawrence Schug

NORTH STAR PRESS OF ST. CLOUD, INC.

Printed in the United States of America by Versa Press, Inc., East Peoria, Illinois.

Published by:
North Star Press of St. Cloud, Inc.
P.O. Box 451
St. Cloud, Minnesota 56302

The following poems were originally published in the listed magazines:

"One Hundred Hawks" and "My Wife and the Snake," *Rag Mag,* vol. 11, no. 1, 1993.

"Bears" *Plainsongs,* vol. 11, no. 2, 1991.

"Owl," *Studio 1,* 1992.

"Interior Decorator," and "Firemaker," *Studio 1,* 1993.

"Black Snake," *Studio 1,* 1991.

"Walkin' the Dog," *Lower Stumpf Lake Review,* vol. XXVI 1991.

"Copper Harbor Cemetery," *Loonfeather,* vol. 13, no. 2, 1992.

"A Visit to Mother's," "Bearing," and "Overpopulation," *Sidewalks,* no. 4, 1993.

"Circle Maker," *Sisters Today,* 1993.

"The Home Team," *Fan Magazine,* no. 10, 1992.

"Cartucho Flower," *Sidewalks,* no. 5, 1993.

"Barbershop," and "Oatmeal," *Sidewalks,* no. 2, 1992.

"The Demolition of St. John Cantius School," *North Coast Review,* Fall, 1993.

"(Agnostic Driving Over) Hills" and "A Letter to Jesus from Paul in the Stearns County Jail," *the Small Pond Magazine of Literature,* vol. 28, no. 3, 1991.

"Breakfast at the Cross River Cafe," *Trestle Creek Review,* no. 11, 1993.

"A Rodeo Prayer," *Lower Stumpf Lake Review,* 1990.

"Baseball," *Sidewalks,* no. 5, 1993.

"Art Exhibit," *the Small Pond Magazine of Literature,* vol. 27, no. 3, 1990.

"Nail Poem #4," and "Nail Poem #2," *Poetry Motel,* no. 19, 1993.

Contents

To Juli

For showing me
little things
and small places

One Hundred Hawks

One hundred hawks
Circle a thermal,
Like Ojibwe dancers
Around a fire.

I dream
One hundred dreams
Of myself
Dressed in feathers.

Bears

I open the glass door of my den,
Wish my nostrils could flare wide,
Assuring me that all is as it should be.
This summer
I will gorge on blueberries
And berrypaint my face.
I'll kiss you with blue lips and
Lick your breasts and belly
With my blueberried tongue.
Next winter you will sleep
In my bed of green and orange moss.
In spring, we will burst
From winter's room,
Crunching crusted snow and
Thrashing through a willow thicket,
The flow within us in flood stage
Because bears know the shortness of summer.

Advice from a Zen Mouse
(For Angie Kocanda)

Honey,
You skitter
Fast as you can
From seed to seed,
Clover leaf to apple peel;
Blanket your bed with chamomile
To sweeten winter's dreams.

Sweetie,
You perk up
Your little pink ears
And twitch your curious nose,
Soften your nest
With feathers and moss,
Lost in a heart of oak.

But listen, darlin',
I thought you ought to know
About the horned-owl's shadow
Gliding over moonlit snow,
About claws and talons and teeth
That snap like traps
On a careless mouse's hide.

So, angel,
Fill your cheeks full,
Oh, yes, baby,
Fill your cheeks full!
There is no birth or death
In this breath,
Only breathing.

Owl

Startled awake by the question,
I lie back, try to settle my heart.
I breathe an owl's song,
Cruise the night on silent wings.

I perch beside my sleeping wife,
Softly feather her cheek,
Whisper that she answers the question
An owl is destined to ask in the dark.

Interior Decorator

The first time I entered her house
A spell settled over me
Like the transparent snake skins
She draped over driftwood,
Mysterious as the empty turtle shell
And the vacant eye sockets
In a mouse-eaten deer skull she'd saved.

She cast a spell of lightning-charred splinters
And tangles of unearthed roots, a spell
That whispers in a vase of feathers
And sleeps in a bowl of river rocks.
Her spell decorates my soul. I gather it around
Like I pulled a thick quilt over my head
Against a cold, bare room where I once lived.

Firemaker

Twenty-five below zero this morning,
Firewood splits easy.
Even the twisted elm snaps,
Oak pops like a gunshot.
My breath coalesces into iceballs
That ornament my mustache,
Glisten in horizontal winter light.
The dog's got his nose in the snow,
Sniffing out voles under the bird feeder.
Not bothered by the cold, he snorts and paws,
Though the voles, smarter than he or I,
Are somewhere underground in a bed of grass,
Nestled and warm as a pile of sleeping puppies.

I picture you beneath a pile of quilts.
I know your skin is warm. I think
That if I make enough noise kicking off my boots,
Filling the woodbox and stoking the stove,
You'll waken and ask me how cold it is,
And when I tell you 25 BELOW, you shiver.
Then I see a thought turn to a smile
In your eyes and you say, Come on back to bed,
Firemaker.

A Day Made Ready

I wake early, rise to prod
Embers back into flame.
I swoosh them with air, some bellowed,
Some my own breath.
I pile sticks, then logs on the fire
Carefully, the way a poem is kindled.

The sleepers in this house,
When they wake, will be pulled
Magnetically, hypnotically, reflexively
Toward the warmth, with hands extended,
Into a new day's open arms, made warm
For them like a cup of breakfast tea.

Bird

I flitted around you
the summer I was a sparrow,
followed you to the river, unnoticed,
feeding on seeds in the words you dropped;
at night, a door closed behind you,
so I slept in wet grass,
tucking my head under a wing of smoke.

I hovered around your house
the winter I was a wren,
aching to enter, afraid to brush
frost-heavy wings against your window.
Finally, you saw my fluttering,
cupped me in your hands,
warmed me with your breath,
whispered to me 'til I sang for you.

My Wife and the Snake

you shoulda seen my wife!
she just picks up this snake
in her bare hands,
holds it right behind its green head
and this snake curls around her arm
and smiles sideways at my wife.
my wife exclaims,
oh, look at him, honey,
ain't he pretty!
and look at his little pink tongue
tasting the air around me!
my wife tells this snake
he may live in the garden
if he keeps the gophers out,
but my wife tells the snake
to stay outa the apple tree.
and I'm standing a ways back,
I'm afraid of snakes,
but I mutter to myself,
yeah, and don't tempt me
with no metaphorical fruit, neither.
and the snake smiles sideways
at my wife.

Black Snake

Sunday afternoon, we kicked stones
And picked the shards of shattered agates
From the last gravel road in the township.
We found sandstone, writing rock we called it,
That smudged our fingers with ancient yellow ink.
Basalt, gneiss, gabbro, and granite, all fire-born,
Now the extinguished coals of time, lay basking, aloof,
As we picked through the sand of a Pleistocene beach.

Monday morning, the orange grade stakes were set,
Surveyed with the precision of a grave-digger's eye;
Straight lines, square corners, and proper depth were assured.
The water truck settled summer's dust with mist,
Belly dumpers dumped load after load of base,
Followed by the grader, packer, and twelve-wheeled roller,
All growling until sunset and overtime pay
Reflected in the operators' eyes.

Tuesday morning, the tar went down at seven o'clock.
Yellow dump trucks, loaded with steaming hot mix,
Stood in line to dump their load into the paver
Like honey bees buzzing around the hive entrance
To deposit their oily, black pollen.
The paver spit out tar like a shedding snake
Leaves its skin, while undulating over the hill,
Swallowing every agate and Sunday afternoon in its path.

Walkin' the Dog

It ain't easy hangin' on
To this blue-green world
While it whirls a cosmic
"Walk the dog"
On a thin string of light
Dangling from the sun's finger.

It ain't easy hangin' on;
Not even for trees,
Or whales,
Or air.
People fly off all the time;
Some jump.

Copper Harbor Cemetery

I introduce myself to the dead,
Husbands, wives, sons, and daughters,
Lying beneath this ragged grass,
Short as summer and penisular lives.
Gravestones, worn faceless as winter,
Lean into a wind I feel as time.
The fingers of hemlock roots sift the soil
For the bones of miners and loggers.
The roots reach to Superior
To touch the bones of shipwrecked sailors.

I introduce myself as a poet.
As a poet, I listen to peninsula soil
For stories of abandoned mines,
Lumbered pines, and belly-up trout.
I ask bedrock questions of the dead.
How endless is the forest?
How cavernous is a one-room cabin
After an infant has died?
Can you hear me, dead Spyalla and Pierskalla,
Reciting your names like poems?

Hit and Run

On a cool September night
The moon backlights flying clouds
That dapple the ground black and silver.
A whippoorwill sings, a cricket hums
And I can hear the abbey bells chime,
Each peal, a laughing skinny dipper
Splashing into a black lake.

Suddenly, the mood is spoiled
By the neighbor kid and his friend
As they peel down their driveway,
Screeching tires, and roar around a muddy oval
Eroded in the old alfalfa field.

The machine-gun pop of unmuffled cylinders
Runs all the music off night's highway.
It's too late to re-capture the stillness,
And I wonder if the deer are anxious,
The birds nervous, the moon as angry as I.

Rooms

I walk an old cow path
We've foot-worn into a trail
Through the red oak grove
And the tamaracks in the bog.
Not cold, it's a good day
For deep breathing, deep thought,
A good day for learning lessons.

From tamaracks I learn
To spread my roots wide,
To give up the glory of my leaves,
While the red oaks teach me
To send a tap root deep
And hang on to the part of me
That catches sunlight.

Confused, I breathe deeply,
Raise my limbs to the sky.
I realize earth has a room
For each root and fallen leaf.
The sky has a room
For bare branches as well as leaves
Rattling on uncertain winds.

The Importance of Each Tree Ring

I stand beside a fallen elm
The morning after a storm
Like a mourner at an old friend's wake.
I remember music fluting in its hollow branches,
And I run my hands over bare wood,
That shone silver-skinned in moonlight.
As I cut firewood, I come to realize
The importance of each tree ring,
And I tell you this, Old Elm,
My hands shake with remorse
That my need for warmth drives me
To cut you again and again.

This hawk-sky day glides and circles,
But our destinies collide on the ground
And we both are changed.
Sunlight rekindled in woodfire is sacred heat,
And knowing the full cost of my warmth
I promise you rebirth, Shadow Caster,
When I solemnly sprinkle your ashes
On resting garden ground.
I ask this of you, Root Maker,
Guide me, after I hollow and fall
And continue my own journey
As ashes melting into the earth.

The Bear

I saw my first un-caged bear
As it loped across Highway 61
A hundred feet ahead of my car.
The bear never looked sideways,
Neither at me or away,
Just crossed the road
And vanished in the birches.
I reached the place
Where the bear had been
But there was no sign a bear
Had ever been there.
And as I passed the spot
Where the bear had crossed,
I almost hit the brake
When I suddenly realized that
There would also be no sign
I had ever driven on this road.

My Shadow Is a Beacon

I know who's who, brother owl,
And I know what's what.
This is not the first time
I've seen rabbit's blood
Splashed on new snow,
Or a pheasant's feathers
Scattered among cattails.

Tonight, I feel small and dark,
Unable to hide in moonlight;
My shadow is a beacon
For telescoping yellow eyes.
I answer the owl
With a mouse's question . . .

me?

A Wealthy Man

Today I visited a wealthy man's house,
A large granite house, 125 years old,
With walls thick as a bank vault,
Standing aloof on a hilltop, like an outcrop
Of bedrock, exposed by glacial ice.
Though the rich man only occasionally visits this house,
His retreat from business in New York and London,
This country estate, its drive columned and gated,
Is furnished with fine artwork and antiques,
Period pieces of opulence that provide the rich man
With a comfort found only in age and stone quiet.

On my way home, I passed the houses of many rich people,
Though if you asked them, they would deny the fact,
As if fat cattle, children, thick cornfields,
Maple-basswood forests, wildflowers, mallard-filled swamps
And deer roaming the hills don't count for much,
Certainly not riches.

Parking my rusting pick-up, I realized that my own house
Near a tamarack bog, is the house of yet another rich man.
Here, I am not hungry, not for food or love or warmth of body.
My days are are large bank accounts of autumn colors,
Black-eyed Susans grow here like interest on an investment.
Though my house is small, and it rattles during blizzard winds,
The sofa is torn and the refrigerator rumbles,
My windows are opulent with sunshine,
As much as any rich person could buy.
And thanks to hard work and good accounting
I remain poor enough to live here all year long.

Martin Luther King Day, 1993

We grew
In different gardens,
But we're simmering
In the same stew, now.
If we don't burn
Or boil over
We could be delicious
Together.

Cartucho Flower*

A small Quiché girl
Stands between her brother
And rifles aimed at his head.
She holds a white flower.
All her people hold white flowers.
And while the young Quiché girl
Holds the riflemen hostage
With the cartucho blossom
Pressed to her breast,
Her people peacefully plead
For an end to their repression.

Fire is their answer,
Fire in the village, in the forest.
The young girl's brother
Is set afire before her eyes.
But fire burning in her people's hearts
Will not be extinguished.
The white cartucho flowers they carry
Bloom like sadness and anger
In the scorched soil of their souls.

*After reading *I, Rigoberta Menchu*

A Dry Flood

Oh, blood runs,
Blood flows
On the cobblestones
Of Beirut,
But the sun and warm bricks
Absorb blood,
Turn it brown,
Then swallow it.

The streets are bloated
With blood and hatred.
The feast
Has been unending
Through generations
Of bleeders.

The blood of children,
The blood of women,
So much blood
The dogs don't bother
To stop and smell.
So much blood,
Yet the militiamen
Will not rest
Until the earth is sated.

". . . a dry flood whose passage leaves more cadavers than flowers." Etel Adnan in *Sitt Marie Rose*

Circle Maker

Our spinning planet
With its molten metal core
Hungers for the bones of us all.
Each step we take
Sinks deeper into dust,
And even Red-tailed Hawk, Circle Maker,
Belongs to Earth.
Neither fear nor despair at this truth,
For truth is circular.
Earth gives back what it takes,
Though Earth renames everything.
Red-tailed Hawk renamed as Worm
Worm renamed as Black-eyed Susan
Black-eyed Susan renamed as Buffalo
Buffalo renamed as Lakotah
Lakotah renamed as Bluestem Grass
Bluestem Grass renamed as Wheat
Wheat renamed as Bread
Bread renamed as Bloodmusclebone
Bloodmusclebone renamed as Work
Work renamed as Poem
Poem renamed as Poet
Poet renamed as Red-tailed Hawk,
Circle Maker.

Breast Fed

I think of my mother,
Twelve year's dead,
Understand how, as a woman
She was waitressed until weary
And finally, cashiered to death
By the mercilessness of a life
She embraced like the drunken husband
That she cured with love.
I feel a sadness today,
Deep as an oak tree's roots,
That the very breast
That fed my hungry stomach,
Was cut away from her.
Her womanhood, cancerous, was discarded,
Not even buried with her.
I feel a duty, born of milk,
To stand with all the world's women
Opposing brothers, sons and husbands,
Men who have ransacked their own nests
And forsaken the sacred breasts
Of women and Mother Earth that nursed them.

A Visit to Mother's

You've gone to Redwood Falls
For a three-day visit with your mother.
It seems a good time for me to visit mine.
On the drive to the cemetery
All the unanswerable questions, too late to ask now,
Rise from the dead again,
And I must drive over the speed limit to get past them.

The grass on my mother's grave feels warm on my bare feet.
Her bones lie below me, yet I look to the sky.
I don't know what this means.
I lean against her stone, talk to her
About my poetry, and I laugh out loud.
I tell her that you and I are still in love.
I'm not sure what that means, either, only that it's true.
I think that she knows Mike and I
Are finally acting like brothers again
After twenty years of undriven freeway between us.
And now that I've told Mother how glad I am
That Mike is back in town, maybe I can tell Mike.

I leave the cemetery when the mosquitoes find me.
I imagine the light in the sky over Redwood Falls
Is the same orange peel and fire that burns over St. Cloud.
You and your mother are probably gathering up your things
From the deck and moving into the house to escape the bugs.
You'll talk at the kitchen table into the night. As will I.

Cynthia

(March 6, 1957 - March 16, 1957)

It hurts to write this, Cindy,
But I write it for you, little sister,
Only sister, to let you know I remember
A tiny face that seemed to smile at me
And a tiny pink hand wrapped around
The tip of my smallest finger,
The only time I saw you alive,
An angel in a hospital crib.

Cynthia, since your tiny pink body,
Fragile as an April daffodil,
Expired with an enlarged heart,
Your small body, dressed in white,
Has lain alone for thirty-six years
In the lowland where the children slumber
Behind the grave digger's shed.
Never to sleep with the mother and father
Who gave you the few heartbeats and breaths
That were the sum of your day-lily life.

This poem is also for me, oldest brother,
Brother who bleeds on paper,
Brother cursed and blessed at once
With the task of drawing water from the well
Of memory and splashing it on my face.

Bearing

She bore six sons,
One for each handle
Of her coffin.
Three left hands,
Three right,
Never clung so tight
To anything.

Game One
Twins 5, Braves 2

A last-place finish brings an early winter.
But this Minnesota summer stretches into October
Like a first baseman scooping a low throw.

Gagne muscled a three-run shot off Leibrandt
And Big Herbie parked one of Pena's fastballs upstairs.
With Morris on the mound in his home town
I had a good feeling about the game, secure
As Sunday mornings when I was a boy.
You were a new father, and sober.
We tossed a baseball back and forth,
Unspoked love, wrapped in horsehide.
"Catch the ball with both hands," you said.

I did what you said, and I have learned
That's the best way to catch everything.
And I'm still hanging on to the ball, Pa.

Game Two
Twins 5, Braves 2

You finished last the year before,
Same as the Twins and the Braves,
But that grin on your face, that day
Back in sixty-two was the same
As Leius wears—a rookie circling the bases
In the World Series.
I remember determination in your eyes,
Buring like the fire in Aguilera's eyes
As he struck out the side in the ninth.
You struck out your devil three times,
Not about to let your game get away
Promising you could give up the bottle.
You swore you weren't going to let your fans down.
And when I think about the first day you went to work
In your one-man barbershop
With its single throne of scrolled brass,
Porcelain and worn leather,
That little room with unmatched chairs
And magazines that were never renewed,
I think you must have felt that finally life
Had put you two games up in your own World Series.

Game Three
Braves 5, Twins 4

Game Three recalled a night thirty years ago
That stretched into extra innings
For the fans outside your hospital room,
A night of pacing, sitting, jumping up,
Then pacing some more; a night spent
Pondering every possible scenario,
Like Kelly and Cox in their dugouts.

I held my breath and prayed inside myself
As one doctor followed another into your room
Like pinch hitters off the bench
Or relief pitchers from the bullpen
Who kept your death off the scoreboard
For at least another inning.

The game developed lke a plot
Unresolved 'til a novel's final page;
No clues given that Mark Lemke,
A most unlikely player, would win the game
After booting a sure double-play grounder
In the top of the twelfth inning.

The lesson learned from your near death
Is the lesson of a baseball game.
Get right back up after a knock-down pitch,
Glare back at that sonofabitch firing fastballs,
Then take a roundhouse swing for the fences.

Game Four
Braves 3, Twins 2

I

The action took place at home tonight.
Brian Harper got knocked on his ass
By Lonnie Smith, a bus without brakes,
But Harp bounced back up, still holding the ball.
Then he dove to stop Morris' wild pitch
And belly-flopped to tag Pendleton at the plate
And keep the Twins in the game.

II

You never laid a hand on Mother,
But you bowled her over hard.
She took a lot of hits for the team,
Retrieved all your wild pitches
And kept your backsliding ways
From crossing home plate.

But there were times, like even Brian Harper,
That she couldn't keep every runner on third.
Now in December, it doesn't matter
Who won or lost the game. What I remember
Is Mother getting back up, time after time,
Just like you, Pa; and just like me.

Game Five
Braves 14, Twins 5

A baseball game of shaking heads and swearing,
This game was all your falls off the wagon,
The jobs lost and chances you squandered.
It was both your amputations
And all your heart attacks put together,
Nine innings of two A.M. phone calls,
Nine innings of "code blues"
And a priest talking slow like a pitching coach.

But for all the time coach Such spent on the mound,
Pitchers West, Leech, Bedrosian, and Willis
Were ineffective as the doctors
Hovering around your bed.
But your fans never hung their heads in doubt.
You said you weren't dead yet and,
By God, you're coming home to play another game.

Game Six
Twins 4, Braves 3

Kirby Puckett's the train
That hauled the load tonight, Pa.
Kirby rapped a single, a triple
and a homer to win it in eleven.
Kirby had three RBIs, a stolen base
And a sacrifice fly.

In the third inning, Atlanta threatening
And Game Five still alive
Behind the home fan's eyes,
Kirby leapt high in left-center,
Near Tony O.'s number six,
And pulled back Gant's home run.

There were no newspaper photos
Of you jumping high,
Snatching back your life
When your game seemed lost.
But there were high-fives and smiles
In your dugout, Pa.

I remember you crossing home plate,
Six little boys running to greet you,
And leaping on your back.
You broke out of your slump and
You were strong enough for extra innings,
You carried the team again.

Game Seven
Twins 1, Braves 0

Jack Morris
Is tough as you were, Pa.
Jack's got balls, Jack's got guts,
Jack's got ten goose eggs
Lined up on the scoreboard
The way you hung zeros
On your scoreboard, ten years
of shutout ball against the whiskey.

Jack Morris
Pitched in and out of trouble
Like the way you came back
From half a dozen heart attacks.
Jack was hot, Jack was cool,
And the knot in my gut
Hasn't unraveled yet,
Though winter covers
Graves and ball fields alike.

Barber

Seven baseball seasons have passed
As fast as stolen bases
On the kitchen radio
Since my father died.
I remember how afternoon sun
Polished his brass barber chair
While another radio ballgame
Crackled to an end.

My father was, at best,
A singles hitter,
But he came to bat
Ready for a curve ball
And managed to get the hits
That kept us in the game.

A poet's words are worth
No more or no less
Than a decent haircut
Or a base hit,
But I hope my turn at bat
Is steady as my father's hands
After forty years of cutting hair—
Worth a home run to some bleacher bum.

Barbershop

It wasn't only the Beatles,
It was the bottles—
Whiskey behind the Wildroot,
Bourbon behind the Brylcreem,
That shut the doors on my old man's shop.
But my old man's face went white
That Sunday night in sixty-four
When the mop-tops shook their shaggy manes,
Looking cool as hell, and a generation
Sang, "Yeah, yeah, yeah."
He closed his eyes in disbelief
And shook his balding head, "No, no, no."
That night, before we went to bed,
My brother and I and a million other kids
Washed the Butch Wax from our heads.
Forever.

The Demolition of St. John Cantius School

Each morning before school,
Our fasting, empty stomachs,
Were force-fed Latin hymns
By the mouthful, whole breakfasts
Of requiem chants, washed down
With the smell of incense. After Mass,
Those of us who received Communion
Were allowed to eat breakfast
At our desks, while those sinners,
(What else could they be?) who'd eaten
Breakfast at home, had to study
Their catechism questions.
During school, we sang church songs,
In English or German, lead by a nun
In full habit. These hymns tasted
Familiar as the summer sausage on
Wonder Bread sandwiches that Mom wrapped
In wax paper early each morning.
On Friday afternoons, after lunch,
Like a not-too-sweet desert
Or a piece of fruit, but not like
Candy or an apple dumpling, we were
Allowed a taste, a nibble
Of some old American song
Like *Oh Susanna* or *Suannee River.*

But Lord A'mighty, when the school bell rang
And the last hymn was sung,
We gorged ourselves on rock 'n roll.
We ate like little pigs at the trough
Of American Bandstand, ate rock 'n roll

Till our bellies ached and our eyes watered.
Songs filled our cheeks, spilled
From our mouths, and we threw up
Those Latin hymns. We stuffed ourselves
On car radios full of static, juke boxes,
Or an old record player's scratchy notes.
And late at night, still not sated,
We wolfed down another tune
Or two before we fell asleep
With a single, small earphone stuck
In our heads, a faint back beat
Spilling out, like cookie crumbs
On the blankets. We went to sleep,
Like every night was Fat Tuesday.
Tomorrow, the cafes would be closed
And the organ would play a funeral dirge.

After Uncle Emil's Funeral

You sat in your one-horse hometown bar
As darkness settled in the car outside,
Where you left your two young sons behind,
Squirming in stiff Sunday suits
And hard shoes.
                                        We were boys.
We didn't understand that sometimes
A man can feel so bad inside,
That the only way he can feel better
Is to make himself feel worse.

A Photograph of Grandpa

Elm shadow, full on stucco house,
Curtains closed against sun,
Grass in sidewalk cracks—
All speak of summer.
The year is 1947, a Sunday, I'd guess
By the white shirt, the tight necktie.
The old man's coat is off in the heat
But he keeps his sleeves cuff-linked.
He wears a straw hat, its brim
Wide enough to shade his face,
When only a noon-length shadow
Dozes on the lawn behind him.

One of my aunts says the old man
Was a hard old son of a gun,
And hints he was worse than that.
But one Sunday he softened,
Stood proudly on the sidewalk
And allowed someone to take his picture.
I'm told the baby he's holding is me.
I don't remember him; he died
Before the roots of my memory took hold.
His railroad watch was passed to Ma, then me,
Perhaps along with the tendency
To seek shelter in shade I make myself.

Lookout Mountain

I remember one time
When Daddy came home
From working out of state
On a power line crew and
I begged him to tell me
About Tennessee, and he
Told me about Lookout Mountain.
Said you can see seven states
From up on its peak.

In an old photograph,
Some people standing on a mountain top.
The only person I recognize is Mother,
Her face smiling, pretty and young.
I don't know which state she's facing
Or how far she can see from there and then.
I want to warn her, "Look out, Mother!"
Though I know she can't hear me.
Her vista is like mine,
Limited as a black and white
Photograph from the past.

don't gimme no

don't gimme no drum machine
don't gimme no drum machine
don't gimme no drum machine
gimme a real guy
in back of a band
beatin' out the blues
on real drums
sweatin' out the blues
on real skin
real guy
real sweat
real blues
real poem

real poem
real blues
real sweat
a real guy
on real skin
sweatin' out the blues
on real drums
beatin' out the blues
in back of a band
gimme a real guy
don't gimme no drum machine
don't gimme no drum machine
don't gimme no drum machine
don't gimme no drum machine

don't gimme no drum machine
don't gimme no drum machine
don't gimme no drum machine
gimme a real guy
in the back of a band
beatin' out the blues
on real drums
sweatin' out the blues
on real skin
real guy
real sweat
real blues
real poem

real poem
real blues
real sweat
real guy
on real skin
sweatin' out the blues
on real drums
beatin' out the blues
in the back of a band
gimme a real guy
don't gimme no drum machine
don't gimme no drum machine
don't gimme no drum machine

(Agnostic Driving over) Hills

Driving over the folds of a country road,
I wonder, at the base of each hill,
If a milk hauler's silver tanker,
With an American flag hanging in the cab,
And the radio playin' Hank Jr.
Has drifted to the wrong side of the road
On the far side of the same hill
I'm climbing in a small, white car,
Singing along with Elvis,
"Return to sender, address unknown."

Free Throw

In Catholic school I was taught
Everyone gets one last shot,
A free throw, with no time left
On the scoreboard clock,
And even if you're losing badly,
This shot can win the game.
But if your Act of Contrition
Is not a perfect "swish"
Your soul will bounce off heaven's rim
And be left, alone and motionless,
On the dark gymnasium floor
After the janitor turns out the lights,
Locks the door, and heads home to heaven.

A Letter to Jesus from Paul in the Stearns County Jail

Jesus,
I've got greasy chicken and cold spuds
lumpin' up in my gut;
I'm ready for sleep, a dream;
I could use a smoke.
It's Sunday, soft time,
hard-thinkin' time.
The other boys are quiet, too.
Last night's drunks are sleeping it off.

Jesus,
I was damn near asleep
when a Salvation Army band shuffled in,
two uniformed women, two uniformed men,
singing "What a friend we have in Jesus."
They stared at the floor while they sang,
wouldn't look in anybody's eyes.
Jesus, what do they know about you?

But, Jesus,
there's a look on the tuba player's face,
and the way he bends his knees
when he bottoms out,
it's enough to make me think
I just might have a friend;
but, Jesus,
we knew when we signed the martyr clause,
that you don't bail nobody's ass out of jail;
not Pete or Andy or Tom. Not Paul.

Paul

The New Hampshire Primary

Dog after dog
Sniffs the snowbank,
Then lifts his leg.
They smell the Presidency!

Oatmeal

I ate breakfast with a friend
Shortly after he'd learned the value
Of thoroughly chewing food.
How nutrients are better digested
When food is thoroughly chewed—
Even oatmeal;
Which I slurped,
Leaned back and burped,
While my friend, contemplative,
Was counting in his head.

Thirty, forty, fifty,
Swallow, dip,
Thirty, forty, fifty,
Swallow, dip,
Deliberate as a banker
Counting money,
As zen as flowing honey.

Now, years later, at the post office,
When I meet this friend,
Our conversations are stretched
As that oatmeal breakfast.
During gaps of silence
We shuffle our feet,
We shuffle our mail,
We chew each other's words
Thirty, forty, fifty times or more
Before we swallow them.

Breakfast at the Cross River Cafe

It's loud as a crow convention
Out front where the locals sit
Cawin' over coffee, black.
Four or five people talk at once,
But somehow everyone listens
To everybody else and the laughs
Spread like maple syrup spilling
From a stack of pancakes.

The tourists sit in the rear,
Cloth napkins in their laps,
Couples talk quietly over decaf
And respect each other's space.
The tourists eat like sparrows
Pecking politely at a feeder
And nobody lets egg yoke
Run over their hash browns or toast.

Nail Poem #11
(Separation)

Boards weather,
Warp over time,

It's not the nail's fault
That the house falls apart.

Highway Red

His face is fifty, so's his belly,
But his strut is twenty-five
And get outa my face, Jack.
I picture him comin' at me;
A low-rider, black-gloved hands
Hung high, twistin' a throttle in the sky.
He wears a black cap backwards
To keep his red hair out of his red eyes,
Set in a sun-skun face, wind red, highway red.

This biker carries grocery bags
Piled high as his crooked barroom jaw,
Close to his barrel chest, his barrel heart.
Bending down low, he whispers to his mother,
Kerchiefed, caned, holding tight to his arm.
He purrs and whispers in her ear,
Rough as his Harley idles;
They ride the city bus, not talking,
Same as he rides empty highway.

The Puppeteer

The hospital corridors, crowded with beds and wheelchairs, narrowed as I walked deeper into a labyrinth of hallways. I felt I was dreamwalking through the stark light and stiletto shadows of a Hesse novel. Time had become fog. Faces, wide-eyed with fate, looked up at me and spoke their names. All spoke my name. Masked technicians moved gloved hands over the dials of monitors blinking red and green and blue. I found a small room and took my seat as the only member of the audience to this surreal production.

Then I heard a voice, a voice worthy of the stage, growing louder as it neared. She whirred into the waiting room, spun circles and figure eights with a twist of her wrist on the wheelchair's controls before she announced herself to the receptionist.

"Rebecca Journelle. J-O-U-R-N-E-L-L-E. Journelle; the e on the end is silent. Some people say Journelli; it's Journelle. The e is silent."

Rebecca Journelle, with the silent e, was no mime by any means. She began her choreography of the uniformed dancer, sending the young volunteer scurrying, and she repositioned the nurse in a long wall of files. Rebecca was quiet for a moment. She turned to me. I felt the tug of strings as my eyebrows, lips, and fingers twitched, and I understood that this was puppet theatre and I was no longer in the audience. The deformed puppet master, Rebecca, a black-shawled, hunch-backed amputee, dubbed me Sir, Kind Sir. Her hands were useless, dried leaves, but her radio voice pulled strings so that my fingers did a wonderful, nimble dance with coins fished from her purse and a can of Diet Pepsi that I held to her contorted lips.

Her name was announced on a loudspeaker, pronounced correctly, and she whirred away without a word. The strings fell away from my limbs, and I slumped back in my chair. I stared at the door, then at my hands, as if they were green leaves.

A Rodeo Prayer

(for Howdy White)

Lord,
Let these broncos and Brahmas
Buck with all the power and grace
You have knotted into their muscle;
Let these rodeo ponies run
Like unfenced prairie wind.

Lord,
Lay your hands on the shoulders
Of sore-assed cowboys;
Guide them safely to the horn;
May their ponies run smart,
May their lassos fly true.

And, Lord,
When cowboys lose their grips
Or their ropes catch only sky,
When cowboys fall, let there be clowns
To scoop them from Adam's dust
And saddle them up to ride again.
Amen.

Nail Poem #4
(state-sponsored rehab)

we lie in forgotten coffee cans,
bent and rusty, with cockeyed heads.
we wait to be hammered straight,
but we fear another pounding.

Baseball

I made it to the Bigs my rookie year.
Smooth as a thoroughbred's hide,
I shone like a new colt in th sun.
I fet the caress, the rough massage
Of a big southpaw's hands, fingers dusted with rosin.
The lefty turned me over and over,
Then gripped me in a fastball grip.
I whistled ninety miles an hour past the batter's stick.
The batter swished; I thumped in the catcher's mitt.
On the second pitch, I dipped and swerved
And left the batter cussin' at my dipsy-do-dah dance.
The third time the fireballer threw me straight down the pipe;
Last thing I remember was a solid crack
Like a whip on horsehide, and I flew, a round Pegasus,
Into the blue heaven above centerfield.
Thirty thousand heads turned to follow my flight;
Even the centerfielder stopped running and watched me
Clear the fence and come to rest in the upper deck.
A red-haired kid in a Twins cap
Held me above his head as the bleacher bums cheered.

I spent that night in a boy's hands, rolling over and over,
Until he slept and dreamed red-headed dreams of his turn
at bat.
Next morning the red-haired kid took me to the sandlot
Where I flew between boys, back and forth, thunk-a-thunk,
Feeling the eternity in boys and baseball games.
I singled, I doubled, I tripled. I homered.
I was a grounder, a fly, a run, a hit, an error.
So the summer passed, and at night I slept
Nestled in the pocket of a Kirby Puckett autograph glove,
(There's no place safer) on a dresser-top covered with
baseball cards.

By August my skin was rough and cut up as a dray horse.
My stitches broken, my hide whirred with every pitch,
Before long those boys wrapped me in electrician's tape and
Pastured me in the sun around the mound with the other old
balls.
Now I sleep on the garage floor with the cracked bats and
The flat gloves the big brothers left behind.
"Yessir, when I was young," I tell 'em,
"I was a fastball that could sing, and I was a rainbow curve,
I was a homerun, upper deck, centerfield, in the Bigs."

Art Exhibit

First I would build a wall of snow
eight feet tall by twenty feet long, facing south.
I would smooth the wall's face
till it was flat as winter sky;
then I would carve nooks in this white wall,
each the size of a bell or a bird.
I would carefully run water over the face of the wall
so that it caught sunlight and moonlight in prisms;
In the nooks I would place brass bells and birdseed,
and, as the lights of night and day cavorted,
I would photograph the wall.
Wrens and finches, unwitting actors,
would sing and kick seed
as the bells became torches of brass.
I would place patio furniture in snow,
(far enough away so that no shadows fell on the exhibit),
where art lovers and foxy uptown women, dressed in pink,
could drink red wine and whisper about light and concept;
and when they were all good and drunk,
I would water them, freeze them in place
to admire my art until Spring.

Nail Poem #2
(single mother)

been hammered on,
pounded on, honey.
my head may be achin',
but I'm the one
holdin' this house together.

Sunday

After church and micro-waved chicken,
Retired farm couples
Drive country roads in blue sedans.
The women in the back seats
Talk about Father Miller's sermon
And how these town girls dress for church.
Two men with lifetime passes to the front seat
Listen to a ballgame crackle on the radio.
Don't say much, don't need to;
They nod at a meadowlark's song and
Smile at the symphony of a baling machine.
There's an old John Deere in the next field;
It sounds like grouse taking flight.

This apartment in the retirement home
And a Sunday drive through Saturday
Are the fruits of fifty years of callouses
And a back that's always sore.
It seems a poor harvest.
Kicking off his shiny Sunday shoes,
The farmer sits on the edge of a bed
In a room that has no window and
A door with two locks.
He wonders about Monday,
with no work to wrap calloused hands around.

A Minnesotan and A Fly

I could've smashed it against the window,
Could've caught that fly bare-handed, easy,
Shook that fly till it was dizzy,
Flies are so slow in January.
But I looked past the fly,
Snow flew outside, I shivered.
The little bugger began buzzin'
Like it thought January was July.
I listened to a peaceful summer song,
Sung acapella, closed my eyes, saw green.
The fly flew away toward an overhead light,
A poor substitute for summer sun,
But, like me, that fly finds summer where it can.

Overpopulation

The deer, this year,
Are thick as poets
In Minnesota.
Still, I haven't the heart
To shoot one—
Deer, that is.